Little Monkey's BIG Peeing Circus

Little Monkey's
BIG
Peeing Circus

By Tjibbe Veldkamp

Illustrated by Kees de Boer

Abrams Books for Young Readers
New York

Little Monkey had a little peepee.
He showed it to Mimi.

"I can *pee* really well," he said.
"I think I'll start a circus."

Little Monkey set up a circus tent.
  "I can pee too," said Mimi.
"May I be a part of it?"

"No," said Little Monkey. "I can *pee* better than anyone.
But when I do my performance, you can stand in the circus ring with me."

From that day on, Little Monkey put on his show— Little Monkey's Big Peeing Circus. Mimi stood on the side.

All the animals from the neighborhood came to watch.

"Ladies and gentlemen," said Little Monkey. "One, two, three . . ."

And then he peed.

"Bravo!" the animals cheered. "Excellent peeing, Little Monkey!"

At every show Little Monkey did a new trick.
He peed very far.

He peed very high.

He peed
standing on
one leg.

And he peed standing on
a chair with his hands in the air.

Mimi had had enough. She didn't want to watch from the sidelines any longer.
She wanted to be part of the show.

Little Monkey put a chair on top of a table.
If he climbed on top of it, he could pee very far down.

"Hey, Little Monkey," said Mimi.
"Have you seen my peepee?"

Little Monkey took a close look at Mimi.

"Your peepee is gone," he said.

"Don't you want to look for it?" asked Mimi.

Little Monkey started to look.

Little Monkey looked here . . .

And there . . .

And there . . .

And here. He searched the entire circus.
But he couldn't find Mimi's peepee.

The audience laughed. First softly. But then much louder.

"Why are you laughing?" asked Little Monkey. "This is not funny! Mimi's peepee has disappeared!"

"I tricked you!" said Mimi. "I don't have a peepee."

"But then you can't pee!" cried out Little Monkey.

"Oh really?" said Mimi. She climbed on top of the chair that stood on the table and said, "Ladies and gentlemen! One, two, three . . ."

Mimi peed.

"Without a peepee!" cried out Little Monkey. "That is very clever!"

"Without a peepee!" cheered all the animals. "That is very clever!"

From that day on, Mimi and Little Monkey performed together.

They could both pee better than anybody.

Designer: Celina Carvalho
Production Manager: Alexis Mentor

Library of Congress Cataloging-in-Publication Data has been applied for.
ISBN 10: 0-8109-3949-5
ISBN 13: 978-0-8109-3949-3

Printed and bound in Singapore
10 9 8 7 6 5 4 3 2 1

harry n. abrams, inc.
a subsidiary of La Martinière Groupe
115 West 18th Street
New York, NY 10011
www.hnabooks.com